Brandon and The Bipolar Bear

Revised Edition

A Story for Children with Bipolar Disorder

Written by Tracy Anglada
Illustrated by Jennifer Taylor and Toby Ferguson

I don't know why, but I'm sad.
I don't know why, but I'm mad.
Can you offer me a hand?
Can you help me understand?
Cheryl Dunham

A Note From the Author

A friend of mine once told me, "The more we know, the better we do." I believe this to be true of parents, like myself, who are struggling to raise children with bipolar disorder. I also believe it to be true for the children themselves. It is to help these children "know more" that I have written this story. My sincere wish is that, along with education, it will also bring hope, understanding and courage to these young hearts and minds.

Brandon is a fictitious character representing children with bipolar disorder. This is not a medical or diagnostic guide. It is a story from my heart to yours. Thank you to Andrew Randall for editing assistance. Also, special thanks to Barbara Giberson, Jennifer Taylor, Patricia and Toby Ferguson, and my loving family for their support.

Tracy Anglada

Brandon and the Bipolar Bear - Original black and white booklet format © Copyright 2001, Tracy Anglada
Brandon and the Bipolar Bear - Colorized Edition © Copyright 2004, Tracy Anglada
Brandon and the Bipolar Bear - Revised Edition © Copyright 2009, Tracy Anglada
All rights reserved.
ISBN: 978-0-9817396-3-2
Library of Congress Control Number: 2009905031

No part of this publication may be reproduced, stored in a retrieval system, or transmitted, in any format or by any means, electronic, mechanical, photocopying, recording, or otherwise, without the written prior permission of the author.

Published by BPChildren
Murdock, FL
United States of America

"MAMA! Mama!" Brandon shouted into the dark room from his hiding spot underneath the covers. He hoped his mother would hurry.

In a flash, there she was, standing right in front of his bed. Brandon sighed with relief as he felt the warmth of her presence.

"What's the matter?" his mother asked. Brandon could see the worry on her face. Or was she angry? It was hard for Brandon to decide. Even when people said they weren't mad, they looked angry to Brandon.

"Uhm ... I ... I need a drink of water," said Brandon.

"You've already had two drinks of water," Brandon's mother said sternly. "Now it's time to go to sleep,"

"BUT Mom, I saw really bad things in my dream again," said Brandon, trying not to sound as scared as he really was.

His mother's voice softened and she sat on the edge of his bed. "I'm sorry you have such bad dreams. If you get scared, just hold on tightly to your new bear."

After a kiss on the forehead and a gentle squeeze, Brandon's mother left the room, which seemed darker now somehow.

'There it is again,' he thought, 'that uncomfortable feeling.' It was always there, but it seemed worse whenever he was alone.

"Maybe I can reach it this time," he said out loud, talking more to himself than to his bear.

BRANDON felt along the front of his pajamas, searching for the tag that must be out of place. Something always felt like it was rubbing the wrong way, no matter what he wore.

'If only I could get it turned around somehow,' thought Brandon, 'then maybe I won't be so sad.' But the harder Brandon tried to reach the tag, the more frustrated he became. It was no use.

"Nobody knows how I feel," grumbled Brandon as he clung to his bear.

A small teardrop fell on the bear's white fur. Then a whole flood of tears fell one after another. Brandon's eyes stung from the tears that just wouldn't stop. His head pounded, and he couldn't remember a time he ever felt worse. But he couldn't remember a time he ever felt better either. As Brandon finally drifted off to sleep, he wondered if he would ever feel good again.

SUNSHINE came pouring in through the blue-and-white-striped curtains hanging in Brandon's window. As the light entered Brandon's room it seemed to chase away the dark, lonely night. But Brandon did not wake up. The birds were singing their morning song outside the window. But Brandon did not wake up. Brandon's mother called from the kitchen. But Brandon did not wake up. Finally, his mother pulled the covers off him and patted his arm.

"Brandon! Brandon! It's time to wake up," his mother said.

"No!" shouted Brandon as he angrily pulled the covers over his head. Brandon clenched his teeth together until his mouth hurt. 'She can't make me get up! I will stay here if I want,' he thought. 'I am never getting out of bed.'

"Come on, sleepy head," said Brandon's mother. "We are going to be late for your appointment."

"I'M NOT GOING!" he screamed as loudly as he could. Brandon could feel the heat of anger rising inside him. It was boiling like the inside of a volcano. 'That's what I am now,' he thought, 'a volcano!'

Brandon knew he was losing control again, and he was afraid. Then, suddenly, he felt something explode inside. Brandon heard himself yelling, but couldn't stop himself. He kicked the bed hard, but it didn't feel hard enough. Brandon kicked his bed again and again but, no matter how hard he kicked, it wasn't enough to show how he felt inside. He grabbed his pillow and flung it through the air. Next, he reached for the bear — his new bear — and pulled with all his might. And then it happened.

"I didn't mean to. I didn't mean to," he sobbed. It was too late. There, on the floor in front of him, lay his new bear, torn and twisted. He tried to put it back together, to make things right, but it wouldn't go back. Brandon rocked back and forth on the floor.

"That's me," he said, as the tears stung his eyes. "I'm broken, like the bear. Nobody can fix me." Then all was silent and empty inside.

Brandon felt his mother wrap him in her arms. They rocked together for awhile. She wiped his tears and picked up the bear.

"We will fix this," she whispered. "I promise."

"How, Mama?" Brandon asked. He watched as his mother gently untwisted the bear and bandaged its broken arm.

"Remember what Dr. Marcus, your therapist, told us?" mama asked.

"I keep trying everything he tells me, but it only helps a little," said Brandon.

"Remember, he also said that sometimes we need a little extra help to feel better. That's why I made a special appointment to go back and see Dr. Samuel today."

"Can my bear come too?" asked Brandon.

"Of course he can," his mother smiled.

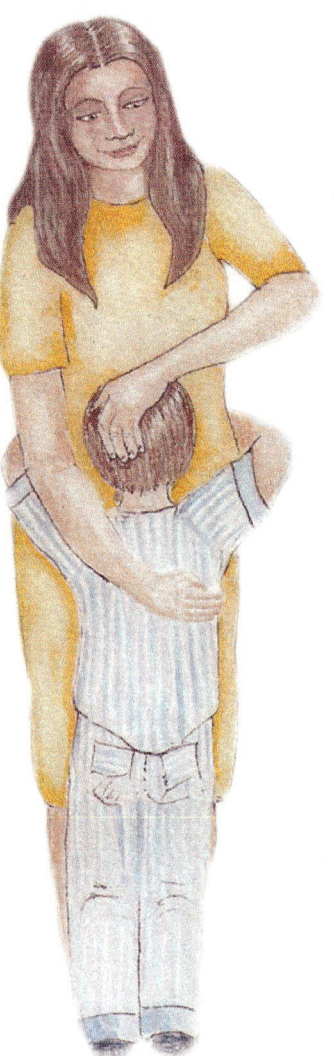

"Hooray! Hooray!" Brandon shouted as he jumped up and zoomed around the room, and then bounced onto the bed laughing.

Up and down he jumped on the bed.

'I'm a rocket,' he thought. 'I will blast off through the ceiling, through the sky, all the way into outer space!'

BRANDON stared at the fish in Dr. Samuel's fish tank.
"Look, Mama! Look! There's a new yellow one this time!" he said excitedly.

"Brandon," Dr Samuel said, "I want to tell you something." Brandon sat close to his mother, careful not to hurt his bear's broken arm. "You have bipolar disorder," the doctor said.

"Bi — what?" asked Brandon as he watched his feet swishing back and forth through the air.

"Bipolar disorder," repeated Dr. Samuel. "You see, people with bipolar disorder have amazing brains that help them do some things really well. What do you do really well?"

"My art teacher says I'm really good at drawing airplanes and rocket ships," shrugged Brandon as he continued watching his feet swish through the air.

"Some of the greatest artists in the world have bipolar disorder, just like you," continued Dr. Samuel. "But having your amazing brain can also create some problems. Bipolar disorder can make your thoughts go too fast sometimes and too slow at other times. It can make you feel full of energy or have no energy at all. It can make your mood feel depressed or too happy, angry or irritable, and anxious or scared. Everyone can feel this way sometimes, but people with bipolar disorder feel these things much stronger and have a harder time controlling their feelings. That's because the way we feel is affected by chemicals in our brain. In people with bipolar disorder, these chemicals can't do their job right so their feelings get all jumbled up inside. That makes it hard to do well in school, make friends and feel good about yourself. I know that you have been struggling with all these things for a while now. It can be scary and confusing. It can be so confusing inside that living seems too hard."

Brandon's feet stopped in mid swing. They were still now, dangling just above the fuzzy carpet.

"I do feel all those things." Brandon stared hard at his new bear, trying to keep his tears from spilling over. "I think I got bipolar because I'm bad," mumbled Brandon.

"Listen to me," said Dr. Samuel. "Many children just like you have bipolar disorder, maybe even a million other kids. Some of them come to see me so that I can try to help them feel better. It doesn't mean that you are bad. You are a good boy with an illness that makes you feel bad inside."

"IF I didn't get bipolar from being bad, then how did I get it?" Brandon asked.

"How did you get your green eyes and your brown hair?" asked Dr. Samuel.

"My Mama has green eyes," Brandon said, looking at his mother.

"And your daddy has brown hair," said his mother as she ran her fingers through his soft hair.

"It's the same with bipolar disorder," said Dr. Samuel. "You can inherit it. Someone else in your family may have it too."

"Will I ever feel better?" Brandon sighed.

"THAT'S the good news," smiled Dr. Samuel. "There is a lot that we can all do to help you. First, your mom and I are going to talk about some medicine that could help you feel better. Next, I'm going to talk to your therapist about working on ways for you to cope when your moods feel too strong. Also, I'm going to send a letter to your school about getting some special tests and extra help in the classroom to make school less stressful for you. You will keep visiting me like before, but a little more often until you feel better."

"Will there be any new fish when I come back?" asked Brandon.

"You never know," smiled Dr. Samuel. Then he looked down at Brandon's new bear. "I sure like your bear. What's his name?" asked the doctor.

Brandon looked at his bear and thought for a moment. "He's a Bipolar Bear, just like me!"

Dr Samuel smiled. "I want you to do one more thing for me, Brandon," he said. "I want you to promise to tell an adult you trust if you ever feel like hurting yourself or letting yourself get hurt. You can tell me or your mom or your teacher or your therapist. None of us will be mad at you. We will do our best to help you."

BRANDON hugged his bear as hard as he could. "I promise," he said. He was sure that if his Bipolar Bear could talk he would say, "Me, too!"

CPSIA information can be obtained
at www.ICGtesting.com
Printed in the USA
LVIC090341140812
294241LV00002BA